Boise State College Western Writers Series Number 2

Mary Hallock Foote

By James H. Maguire
Boise State College

Publication of this pamphlet was made possible by a grant from the Idaho State Commission on the Arts and Humanities

Cover Design by Arny Skov,
Copyright 1972

Illustration, "The Irrigating Ditch," by Mary Hallock Foote from *The Century Magazine*, 38 (June 1889), 298.

Boise State College, Boise, Idaho

Library of Congress Card No. 72-619586

International Standard Book No. 0-88430-001-3

Printed in the United States of America by
The Caxton Printers, Ltd.
Caldwell, Idaho

Mary Hallock Foote

Mary Hallock Foote

IN HER PREFACE TO *The Last Assembly Ball* (1889) Mary Hallock Foote said that "the East generalizes the West as much as England has the habit of generalizing America; taking note of picturesque outward differences, easily perceived across a breadth of continent" (p. 5). Twelve novels and numerous short stories and sketches testify to Mrs. Foote's attempt to avoid such generalization, to see and describe the West with that "Common Vision" which Edwin H. Cady has defined as Realism in American fiction (*The Light of Common Day,* p. 5).

Born and raised an Easterner, Mary Hallock Foote came West armed with sketch pad and pen, and left not only illustrations and prose fiction as records of her experience, but also a 350-page manuscript of her "Reminiscences" (soon to be published). Mrs. Foote's interesting and varied life served Wallace Stegner as model, in part, for *Angle of Repose* (1971), and his novel shows that "contrary to the myth, the West was not made entirely by pioneers who had thrown everything away but an ax and a gun" (p. 41).

In her "Reminiscences" Mrs. Foote describes her early life as being both simple and rich—simple in its rural Quaker setting, rich in education and acquaintance. She was born in 1847 in Milton, New York, not far from the Hudson River. Related, as her father jested, to half the New York Yearly Meeting of the Society of Friends on his side of the family, she could also count the other half of the Meeting as relatives on her mother's side. Little wonder that speakers from the New York Antislavery Society (to which her Aunt Sarah belonged) visited the Hallocks. These visitors, "brilliant talkers," appeared at intervals between 1856 and the Civil War and included such fiery abolitionists as Susan B. Anthony and Ernestine L. Rose. The Hallock children had been well taught to appreciate such visitors: each evening the family, Free Soil Republicans, gathered so that father could read the congressional debates and the editorials in the *New York Tribune*. Friends School in the Old Meeting House and an ample family library made up the balance of Mary's early education.

Such a milieu prepared Miss Hallock for the Poughkeepsie Female Collegiate Seminary. Her education during those years did not derive solely from her mastery of mathematics nor from her associations: three of her young Quaker relatives died fighting in the Civil War while she attended classes. Poughkeepsie was a springboard to the Cooper Union Institute School of Design in New York City, where she developed such a talent as an illustrator that she earned commissions from such firms as Fields, Osgood, and Company (to illustrate some of Longfellow's poems) and from *Harper's Weekly*.

Indirectly, the Cooper was also responsible for Mrs. Foote's career as a novelist, for it was there she met Helena De Kay and Emma Beach. Helena brought such literary notables as Richard Watson Gilder and George Washington Cable to the Hallock home in Milton. Through her friendship with Emma Beach, Mary Hallock met someone quite different from Gilder and Cable. His name was Arthur De Wint Foote, and he was the first cousin of that great friend of the Beaches, Henry Ward Beecher. Foote worked as a civil engineer at Tehachapi Pass and on the Sutro Tunnel, two difficult assignments impressive in a young engineer's dossier.

Such a man as Arthur Foote, fresh from the Far West, must have seemed quite a contrast to the literati whom Mary Hallock met in Boston after Arthur returned to the West. While he was wooing her by mail, she was traveling to "the hub of the universe" at the invitation of A. V. S. Anthony of Fields, Osgood, and Company to meet the "makers of American Literature." Her feelings about the Bostonian laying-on of hands were similar to those of the young William Dean Howells. In figurative terms she said of the approval which men like Longfellow had expressed for her talent, "your shoulders tingled ever after" ("Reminiscences," p. 47). Sensitive though her shoulders were, her heart was even more susceptible to her young Westerner.

After her wedding to Arthur at Milton, Mrs. Foote began her first residence in the West late in the summer of 1876. In that centennial year when Custer met his defeat, Mary Hallock Foote crossed the continent by train with a maid and the maid's baby, and with an order to illustrate a new edition of *The Scarlet Letter* (the maid soon became Priscilla). In San Francisco the trio was welcomed by Arthur and his sister and brother-in-law, James and Mary Hague. In her "Reminiscences," Mrs. Foote said her arrival proved her love for Arthur: "No girl ever wanted less to 'go West' with any man, or paid a man a greater compliment by doing so" (p. 58). However great her reluctance to settle in the wilds of California, she discovered that the "tingling" in her shoulders, remained, that she could still sketch, read, and write. Her illustrations became so highly professional that Regina Armstrong said in *The Critic* (August 1900), "in point of priority, Mrs. Foote may truthfully be called the dean of women illustrators" (p. 131).

California also nurtured her talent as author. To her old friend Helena De Kay and her husband Richard Watson Gilder, she wrote long descriptions of the countryside and the people. As editor of *Scribner's* and later of *The Century,* Gilder quickly recognized the literary possibilities of Mrs. Foote's descriptions. According to Herbert F. Smith, Gilder's editorial policies encouraged regional literature; he wanted his magazine to help create a truly national literature that would combine realism and idealism

(*Richard Watson Gilder,* pp. 86-87). The Gilders asked their friend Mary to work some of her letters into magazine articles.

"A California Mining Camp," based on the Foote's young married life at New Almaden, and "A Sea-Port on the Pacific," descriptions of Santa Cruz where Mary waited while Arthur tried to find a new job, heralded her debut as a writer. She was also new to the business of being a mother—Arthur Burling Foote had been born on April 29, 1877. The next seven years provided the new mother/writer with a great deal of what Henry James called the *donnée* of fiction, but she had little time to create literature with the materials of her experience. During 1878 while Arthur worked for George Hearst at the Homestake mill in Deadwood, South Dakota, Mary took the baby home to Milton. Arthur refused to play Hearst's dirty financial games and found other work in Leadville, Colorado, where his family joined him in 1879. There Mrs. Foote received in her mountain cabin such stimulating visitors as Helen Hunt Jackson, Clarence King, and Thomas Donaldson (author of *Idaho of Yesterday*).

Winters in Leadville, without the summer's company and with temperatures far below zero, had little appeal to Mrs. Foote. In the winter of 1879 she returned to Milton, where she had left her malaria-stricken baby with his grandparents. "All our lives," she wrote in her old age, "we alternated in this way, swinging between two sides of the continent, between safety in the East (where lurked unsuspected germs) and risks in the far places which we recognized and defied" (p. 104). The Footes next swung back to Leadville; a mining dispute arose, and they headed back East. Arthur quit the Leadville job and accepted an appointment to examine some mines in the Michoacan Province of Mexico. He took Mary, and her reports of the trip were published in *The Century*.

Published travel sketches to her credit, Mrs. Foote turned to fiction, with ample time for writing while she waited in the East for Arthur to find a job. After some searching with John Sherman, his wife's brother-in-law, Arthur found a job as Chief Engineer and Manager of the Idaho Mining and Irrigation Company. Mary and her sister, Bessie Sherman, took their children to Boise, Idaho. The years spent in Idaho—1883 to 1895—were, as Mary Lou Benn has put it, "to bring heartbreak, failure, and discouragement" to the Footes ("Mary Hallock Foote: Pioneer Woman Novelist," p. 35). While Arthur fought hard but failed to realize his dreams of great irrigation projects (later built by the Bureau of Reclamation as he had designed them), his wife had to move her family from the Father Mespie house to engineers' headquarters in Boise Canyon, then to the Shermans', and finally to the Mesa.

In 1895 the family moved to Grass Valley, California, where Arthur, on the advice of brother-in-law James Hague, became manager of the North Star Mine. In 1904 the Footes' daughter Agnes died, and though her other children, Arthur and Betty, were there to console Mrs. Foote, her "Reminiscences" stop at this point. Young Arthur, educated at St. Paul's School and M. I. T., and trained in the mines of Korea, succeeded his father as manager of the North Star when the older man retired in 1914.

The Footes continued in retirement at Grass Valley until 1932, when the pendulum of their traveling clock again moved them East, this time to Hingham, Massachusetts. Their daughter Betty lived with them during these last years. According to Mary Lou Benn, "Arthur Foote died in 1934 at the age of 84, but Mary Hallock Foote lived on until the age of 91 with death coming June 25, 1938" (p. 41).

Before her death, Mrs. Foote remarked on a cruel twist of fate that had befallen other writers of the period such as William Dean Howells. She doubted that, without the help of editorial friends, she would ever have another story accepted, "so completely has my vogue passed away" ("Reminiscences," p. 82). That the public had lost interest was as much its loss as Mrs. Foote's, for her skill as novelist grew with her years.

The encounter between East and West, central to most of her works, is most artistically pictured in all its nuances in her later novels. Though not so successful as works of art, her earlier novels are no less faithful in their attempts to show Western life from the woman's point of view. Her early, formative period is separated from the late period by the turn of the century. To trace the development of her work is to watch her refine her conviction that "Socially, it [the West] is a genesis, a formless record of beginnings, tragic, grotesque, sorrowful, unrelated, except as illustrations of a tendency towards confusion and failure, with contrasting lights of character, and high personal achievement" (*The Last Assembly Ball,* p. 7).

Her first attempt to embody this insight in a novel was *The Led-Horse Claim* (1883). George Hilgard, superintendent of the Led-Horse, falls in love with Cecil Conrath, sister of the superintendent of the Shoshone, the mine next to Hilgard's. The tunnels of the Shoshone have been illegally pushed into Led-Horse territory; so trouble between the rival concerns hangs over Hilgard's engagement to Cecil. Tunnels eventually connect, and the Led-Horse barricades the boundary. The two sides shoot it out. Hilgard returns to Cecil with the news that either his bullet or his foreman's killed her brother. The engagement is broken. Hilgard resigns and returns to New York to find another job.

By coincidence, Hilgard stays in a hotel room close to that of Cecil and her aunt. When they learn that he has fallen deathly ill, the two ladies nurse him back to health. Despite this act of charity, Cecil informs Hilgard that their love cannot be realized in this world because of her brother's death. She goes to stay with her grandmother at Little Rest, a rural home built in the early 1800's. She befriends two young boys who are (unbeknownst to her) Hilgard's younger brothers. While Cecil and the boys are skating, Hilgard arrives and the two lovers are reconciled. Cecil's final decision to marry him is still difficult, and the marriage is viewed with some bitterness by her family.

Mrs. Foote later wrote of this first novel, "It told of things that interested the writer [the mining conflict was based in part on her husband's experience] and was called a success; if it was, it was a most ingenuous one" ("Reminiscences," pp. 197-198). In agreement with Mrs. Foote's assessment, Mary Lou Benn said of *The Led-Horse Claim,* "The characters come alive only as types" (p. 51). Mrs. Benn saw five stock characters in the book: hero (Hilgard), heroine (Cecil), protagonist (Cecil's brother), the other woman (Mrs. Denny, who is not a "fallen woman" but is far too loose in conduct), the philosopher (Dr. Godfrey, a convivial confidant of other characters, who manages to see some good in everyone), and the villain (Gashwiler, the man who goads Cecil's brother into his robbery). These stock types too frequently meet as the result of coincidences that fail to convince the reader.

In spite of these weaknesses, *The Led-Horse Claim* presents an emotional dilemma similar in its outcome to the agonized decision made by Penelope and her parents in Howells' *The Rise of Silas Lapham.* Cecil must decide whether to marry a man who might have killed her brother. She opts sensibly and not without anguish to do what seems best for those concerned, rather than to cling to a sentimental notion of sacrificing herself to her brother's memory (dubious at best because he was clearly in the wrong). Mrs. Foote tried to show the complexity and ambivalence involved in making some decisions, just as she attempted to avoid the extremes of character found in melodrama. Dr. Godfrey, determined to credit everyone with some worthwhile trait, is for Mrs. Foote what the narrative voice was for Anthony Trollope in showing the many facets of a single character.

Dr. Godfrey and the other characters also serve to present views about the West. Aware of the artificial, highly transient social life in the booming mining town, Hilgard says, "We are none of us living our real lives" (p. 65). The characters have left behind many of the customs and traditions of the East and must act according to new social rules. As Dr. Godfrey explains of a dance, "Here, there is no classification. You have to pick your way among all the people who are crowding you, elbow to elbow" (p. 91). This fluid social situation, useful to her fiction as a field of ordeal but too unsettled for any resolution, probably prompted Mrs. Foote to place the denouement in the East where she was more certain of social behavior.

She seems far more certain of the special situation of the West in her second novel, *John Bodewin's Testimony* (1886). The use of dialect is a good example of her increased confidence. An Irish maid and a few miners with dialects appear occasionally in *The Led-Horse Claim,* but these characters seem to be there mostly in obeisance to the tradition of such picturesque touches as those which appear in the works of James Fenimore Cooper. Similar characters in *John Bodewin's Testimony* appear in their own right: their dialects are "Western," they occupy a significant portion of the action, and they emerge as something more than "flat" characters (as E. M. Forster used the term).

The difference between her first two novels stems from Mrs. Foote's use of her *donnée.* The action in both novels revolves around incidents based on her husband's mining experience in Leadville. *John Bodewin's Testimony* bears a similarity to the actual court testimony of Arthur Foote. But in that second novel we also find descriptions of mountain scenery, the use of more "common" characters, and fewer comparisons with life in the East. Consider the novel's final passage:

> Wind of the great Far West, soft, electric, and strong, blowing up through gates of the great mountain ranges, over miles of dry savannah, where its playmates are the roving bands of wild horses, and the dust of the trails which it weaves into spiral clouds and carries like banners before it! Wind of prophecy and hope, of tireless energy and desire that life shall not satisfy. Who that

> has heard its call in the desert, or its whisper in the mountain valleys, can resist the longing to follow, to prove the hope, to test the prophecy. (p. 344)

These words evince a recognition of the West's glories in a vein similar to that which Max Westbrook (in his biography of Walter Van Tilburg Clark) has identified as Western Realism. The West appears in this novel as fit gound for ordeals that can lead to "high personal achievement."

John Bodewin's achievement is not without personal sacrifice. He had come to the mines of Colorado in pursuit of a sister who was destitute and alone after her husband's suicide and who was rescued from indigence by Col. Harkins, an unscrupulous mine owner. Though his sister dies, Bodewin remains indebted to Harkins for saving her from a pauper's death. Because Bodewin is an engineer, Harkins compels him to reciprocate by testifying for him in a claims dispute. Bodewin agrees, but then falls in love with Josephine Newbold, daughter of Harkins' rival. Newbold, prone to stacking a deck himself, uses his daughter's new suitor to good advantage: after some ambivalent soul-searching, Bodewin agrees to foresake Harkins and his fraudulent claim and to testify for Newbold.

Harkins and his confederates scheme to thwart the young engineer's new intentions. Jim Keesner, a Harkins man, and his son Tony kidnap Bodewin. They take him to a mountain cabin which had been discovered by friends of Bodewin on a picnic prior to the kidnapping. Hillbury, a member of the U.S. Geologic Survey, had even visited the cabin and found Keesner's daughter Babe in possession of Bodewin's picture. When Hillbury returns to the cabin seeking his kidnapped friend, he sees from a distance that Bodewin, alone with Babe, has her head resting on his shoulder. Although Bodewin escapes, his reputation seems destroyed by what his friend has witnessed. His position is further damaged when Babe, one of Mrs. Foote's most successful renditions of a lower class woman of the West, follows Bodewin back to the mining camp. Out on a piazza watching the occultation of the star Antares behind the moon, Bodewin sees Babe watching Josephine and him, runs after her, and helplessly watches a mine car dump a load of tailings on her. She dies in his arms after making him promise not to tell anyone that he knew her.

That promise binds Bodewin to the web of circumstantial evidence that has been building about him. The climax comes in a trial scene that is very similar to the concluding scene of another regional novel of the period, Edward Eggleston's *The Graysons* (1888) As in Eggleston's novel, there are courtroom surprises, but Bodewin is only further implicated by each additional bit of evidence. His friend Hillbury testifies against him; Bodewin, constrained by his promise, cannot explain that he was only removing something from Babe's eye when Hillbury saw them together. Bodewin's testimony fails to convince the jury; so Newbold loses. After the trial, Tony Keesner tries to shoot Bodewin to avenge Babe's death. His first shot misses, and when Harkins deflects the second, Tony accidentally shoots him. Bodewin, dishonored, leaves. To vindicate himself with Josephine, he writes her the truth and also declares his love for her. Hillbury later visits Josephine, whereupon she shows him Bodewin's letter. She chides Hillbury for deserting his friend: " 'Is it not true,' she said, 'that proofs can lie? The only thing that can be trusted is character' " (p. 338). Moved by the letter, Hillbury goes in search of Bodewin, finds him, and convinces him to go to Josephine and to marry her. After their marriage, the Bodewins return to the mining town.

The couple's return to the West, a contrast to the ending of *The Led-Horse Claim,* provides only one example of Mrs. Foote's growing ease with Western ways and places. Babe, a Daisy Miller of the mountains, emerges as more than the rough servant type, and the mining camp is pictured as a nascent community rather than a godforsaken battlefield in the wilderness. Society apparently did exist in the West of the late seventies; though rules suited the frontier situation, decorum consisted of far more than a claim and a gun.

In fact, *The Last Assembly Ball* (1889) shows how difficult proper social conduct becomes under such circumstances. Fanny Dansken, widowed proprietor of a Leadville boarding house, makes the social life of her young gentleman boarders her personal responsibility. She encourages them to behave better than Boston Brahmins, and she declares the local ladies off limits. Her solicitude, though it does protect the reputation of her establishment, is in the best interests of the young men: "Eastern women may be wanted in the West, but Western women are never wanted in the East. Why? Because there are women enough there already—women who are acclimated, body and soul. And how does it end? You forsake your East for the sake of your wife, or your wife for the sake of your East" (pp. 33-34). In spite of this harsh dictum, necessity forces Mrs. Dansken to hire Milly Robinson, young, beautiful, and a Canadian sufficiently Western to earn her employer's off-limits designation.

Unfortunately for the peace of the boarding house, Frank Emry, a young mining engineer who is in exile because he has been forbidden to marry a girl in the East, falls in love with Milly. With an independence of mind like that of Howells' Tom Corey, Emry brings Mrs. Dansken Jane Austen's works to give to Milly. Again the landlady counsels against any friendship with Milly, but the infatuated Emry forces Mrs. Dansken to this defense of her strictures: "Women are always the judges of women, and men who have any sense accept their judgment. They scold and they sneer at us, but they expect us to keep society in order, while they do as they please outside" (p. 119). When Mrs. Dansken learns that Emry has deliberately defied her by asking Milly to an "Assembly Ball," her angered reaction forces the young couple out of the boardinghouse and into a church.

The new marriage begins under some awesome burdens. Milly is not so virginal as she looks to Emry: Colorado made her a widow, and she had a baby that died. Emry does not learn of her past until after he has taken her to the last assembly ball, where the women snub her and a drunk insults her. The insult precipitates a duel that Emry fights even after he learns about his wife's past. He is shot and dies the next morning. Some time later, Milly marries a Montana cattleman, and Mrs. Dansken takes one of her boarders to the altar.

The story has little of the sentimental. The novel's three-part structure, explicitly dramatic ("The Situation," "The Situation Developed," and "The Catastrophe"), emphasizes the grimly realistic ending. As in the novels of many other American realists, the action stems from character. Though Mrs. Dansken is admirably suited to preside over a salon typical of New York but in the heart of Leadville, she overestimates the power of her advice and forgets the effect of such a pretty face as Milly's. Milly's beauty is not her only weapon; she pretends an innocence both beguiling and deceptive. Deceived as much by his belief in a friendly and permissive Western society as by Milly's supposed innocence, Frank Emry learns too late the observation Mrs. Foote makes in the introduction to the book: "no society is so puzzling in its relations, so exacting in its demands upon self restraint, as one which has no methods, which is yet in the stage of fermentation" (p. 5).

An artist faced especially severe problems in a fermenting society, as Mrs. Foote showed in *The Fate of a Voice* (published in 1889 in the same volume with *The Last Assembly Ball*). Madeline Hendrie comes to the Klamath River valley to visit her sister's family and to breathe the dry Western air that she hopes will eliminate the rasp in her fine singer's voice. Aldis, one of the men working with her brother-in-law on the railroad, falls in love with her and proposes. Unwilling to give up her career in the East, tempted though she is, Madeline replies, "Art is love, without its selfishness" (p. 233). After that pronouncement, she trips and almost falls over a cliff. In saving her, Aldis falls. Madeline, thinking he must be dead, loses her voice altogether. But Aldis falls onto a clump of syringa and survives with little damage.

The loss of her voice should convince Madeline to marry Aldis —at least he thinks so. Though she has nothing more to sacrifice to a Western marriage, the mute singer still refuses; now she says she is not good enough for Aldis. She returns to New York, and after training, regains her voice. Aldis comes East, and this time she sacrifices her career to her love for him. The value of her voice itself is not lost: "the soul of music, wherever it is purely uttered, will find its listeners; though it be a voice singing in the wilderness, in the dawn of the day of art and beauty which is coming to a new country and a new people" (p. 275).

The Chosen Valley (1892) presents the story of a different kind of voice singing in the wilderness, the voice of the professional engineer trying to make straight the way of irrigation projects in Idaho's Snake River valley. The engineers, Robert Dunsmuir and Philip Norrisson, try to develop plans for a strong, well-designed dam that will safely hold enough water to turn the valley floor into fertile farmland. They fight Price Norrisson, Philip's father, a man who also wants to see a dam built but who wants to "make a buck" doing it. The elder Norrisson buys officials, spreads rumors, does anything he must to force Dunsmuir to surrender his water rights. With such a force working against him, Dunsmuir gives up his years-long struggle to find capital and throws in his lot with Price. Philip also joins his father, and the two engineers eventually find they are ordered to build in unsound ways. Tearing up a letter of resignation, Dunsmuir, though he knows he is wrong to do so, decides to remain on the job, because, "It's money that builds here, not brains and education" (p. 291).

The cheaply constructed dam goes out and takes Dunsmuir with it. Repentant and convinced that Dunsmuir was originally right, Price has his son reconstruct the dam according to the first plans. Pleased with his own magnanimous reparation, Price places on the dam a plaque in memory of Dunsmuir. Philip marries Dunsmuir's daughter.

With the exception of an incongruous scene in which Dunsmuir's son is trapped in a lava bed cave with a Mexican bandit, this story manages to illustrate the effect of the American dream in the West. Whether successful or not, fathers find their sons repudiating their beliefs and life styles. Dunsmuir's son wants only to be a cowboy and even publicly mocks his father's engineering dreams in an Independence Day celebration. Norrisson's son is equally disenchanted with his father's goals—Philip's primary aim in life is not money; he wants only to be a good engineer. However, everyone's integrity suffers because means take second place to tempting ends. In his own way each man sees the Western desert as his chosen valley. Philip, for example, is drawn West in opposition to his mother's wishes and without any purely financial need: "A man," says Mrs. Norrisson, "should go East for his education, his accent, and his wife. He may go west for his fortune perhaps; but you do not need a fortune, Philip" (p. 7).

In a remarkable concluding passage, Mrs. Foote explains this irresistible lure which the West exerts on the imagination:

> The ideal scheme is ever beckoning from the West; but the scheme with an ideal record is yet to find—the scheme that shall breed no murmurers, and see no recreants; that shall avoid envy, hatred, malice, and all uncharitableness; that shall fulfill its promises, and pay its debts, and remember its friends, and keep itself unspotted from the world. Over the graves of the dead, and over the hearts of the living, presses the cruel expansion of our country's material progress: the prophets are confounded, the promise withdrawn, the people imagine a

> vain thing. Men shall go down, the deed arrives; not unimpeachable, as the first proud word went forth, but mishandled, shorn, and stained with obloquy, and dragged through crushing strains. And those that are with it in its latter days are not those who set out in the beginning. And victory, if it come, shall border hard upon defeat. (pp. 313-314)

This perceptive, moving statement of the lust to rape the land of its treasures almost compensates for the novel's thrice-repeated narrative and for some of its incongruous episodes.

With all its faults, *The Chosen Valley* presents a more nearly balanced view and a more realistic treatment than *Coeur d'Alene* (1894). In the latter Mrs. Foote seemed to forget what she had written in a letter from New Almaden on November 5, 1876: "Do you think it artistic for a writer to espouse a cause as deliberately as in D. D. [George Eliot's *Daniel Deronda*], and force it on her readers—indeed on her characters too." *Coeur d'Alene* so espouses the cause of Northern Idaho mining companies that Robert Wayne Smith in *The Coeur d'Alene Mining War of 1892* has called the book a "piece of antiunion propaganda" and a "sentimental piece of fiction which twists the facts in order to make the story go" (p. 125). Twenty years after the fact, Mrs. Foote admitted in her "Reminiscences" that "My work at this time was pot-boiling which is 'all right,' Kipling remarked in one of his letters, 'if it boils the pot' " (p. 304). In fact, in a letter from Boise on January 20, 1895, Mrs. Foote told a friend who asked for an autographed copy of *Coeur d'Alene*, "The book seems to me too crude as a novel. . . ."

Perhaps it was crude as a novel, but the book had so pronounced an anti-union effect that in 1906 the National Metal Trades Association of Cincinnati asked Houghton Mifflin (Mrs. Foote's publishers) for permission to serialize it. By then the book had already been translated for the "Bibliotheque Universelle and Revue Suisse" (1899) ; and Mrs. Elizabeth W. Doremus, author of *The Circus Rider* and *Four in Hand,* had dramatized it.

The book lent itself to popular dramatization. Darcie Hamilton, the hero, arrives in the Coeur d'Alene mining district to investigate the management of the Big Horn, a mine owned by his father's British company. Darcie's identity remains concealed from the Americans, but this subterfuge creates a problem when Faith Bingham, daughter of the Big Horn's manager, attracts Darcie's notice and the two fall in love. Their courtship struggles over heartbreaking obstacles: Faith's father, drunken and dissipated, is in collusion with the union; labor gunmen shoot and wound Darcie after tricking him to come to what they said would be a rendezvous with Faith (Bingham's servants sympathize with the union and tell it everything about Faith and Darcie). Unionists seize some mines by dynamiting the management, and troops are asked to quell the disorder. Bingham, cowed by union force, sends a telegram asking that troops not be sent. Miners torture Wan, the Bingham's Chinese servant, to find out where Darcie is, but their efforts are useless. Darcie escapes. Faith also leaves the area on a train with scabs. Many of these refugees, waiting at Lake Coeur d'Alene for steamboat passage, fall victims to a bloody union ambush. Troops arrive and rout the unionists. Survivors of the massacre, Darcie and Faith marry and return to the mines, where Darcie assumes the management of the Big Horn.

The action contains elements that typify Mrs. Foote's early works. The hero or heroine, usually a refined Easterner, falls in love with someone belonging to an opposing faction. This formula serves when the action evolves convincingly from the nature of the characters and the situation. *Coeur d'Alene* suffers from the artist's failure to proceed on those terms; instead, Mrs. Foote attempted to picture the unionists as black-hearted villains totally devoid of humanity in contrast to the reasonable, compassionate mine owners. One passage serves as illustration of Mrs. Foote's failure to comprehend the nature of the miners' movement, their solidarity, and the necessarily grim way they treated scabs: "There was no Traveler from Altruria to ask: Who are these decent poor men [the strikebreakers]? Why have they come here, and why do they go, by a common, sad impulse, as if through fear and force? And if so, who compels them? And what is their offense that they should be looked at askance and herded apart, like tainted cattle? A deeper question, this would be, than most of us are prepared to answer. Even the facts can hardly be trusted to answer; for facts are cruel, and they frequently lie, in the larger sense of truth" (p. 194). In none of Mrs. Foote's later works do the characters seem such wooden stereotypes nor does the action seem so patently contrived to give the author a chance to condemn something like "mob action."

In Exile, and Other Stories (1894) represents Mrs. Foote's growing concern with the effects of the past on the present—she often likened that relationship to a "ground-swell," the delayed coastal consequences of a storm far out at sea. Sins of fathers visited on sons, Eastern manners and cultivated tastes uprooted in the move West, even the lament of *ubi sunt*: whatever form it takes, the ground-swell effect devastates mercilessly and indiscriminately.

"In Exile" answers a question Mrs. Foote had once faced. Mr. Arnold and Miss Newell, both Easterners living in the California mountains, enter upon a general discussion that has bearing on their particular situation. Arnold asks, "Did you ever happen to see a poem or a story, written by a woman, celebrating the joys of a solitary existence with the man of her heart?" (p. 15). Miss Newell suffers considerable disappointment when she learns that Arnold asks the question because he hopes to bring his Eastern financée West after their marriage. The question eventually applies to Miss Newell, however, for Arnold's fiancée refuses him; and some months after he recovers from that blow, Arnold proposes to Frances Newell. She accepts. "They are still in exile,"

Mrs. Foote concluded, saying of the new Mrs. Arnold, who had still not made her first return visit East, "the old home still hovers, like a beautiful mirage, on the receding horizon" (p. 58).

Mrs. Foote used her old home as the setting for "Friend Barton's Concern." Thomas Barton, a Quaker, leaves his wife and family in the summer of 1812 to preach across the land. Upon his return, Barton finds his daughter Dorothy in love with Walter Evesham, son of a colonel who had fought at Saratoga in the American Revolution. Barton does not relish allowing his daughter's marriage to a member of a family so bound to violence, but he relents. Years later, Dorothy's grandson dies at the Battle of Shiloh.

Retribution is also central to "The Story of the Alcázar." Capt. John tells a young lad that in 1827 an old slave ship, the Alcázar, entered Penobscot Bay. The abandoned ship's hold contained skeletons of dead slaves. A Capt. Green re-outfitted the ship, but it crashed into a bar during a storm, and Green drowned. Capt. John says the Alcázar had been Green's ship when it was a slaver and that the ship followed him to avenge the deaths of the slaves. This much of the story Mrs. Foote handled well, but she added a gratuitous touch of sentiment—Green's widow was Capt. John's childhood sweetheart—that offsets the stark effect of the old sailor's yarn.

Like "The Story of the Alcázar," "A Cloud on the Mountain" and "The Rapture of Hetty" contain many of the romantic touches characteristic of such popular works as Anthony Hope's *Prisoner of Zenda,* which appeared in the same year as *In Exile.* "A Cloud on the Mountain" does not, however, lack realism. Ruth May Tully, daughter of a rancher in Bear Valley, Idaho, falls in love with Kirkwood, a young engineer, while her fiancé, packer Joe Enselman, struggles to survive on a mountain. When Joe returns, one of his eyes is gone; Ruth cannot bring herself to say she no longer loves him. Her dilemma ends when she drowns while trying to warn Kirkwood of a flashflood. "The Rapture of Hetty" ends more happily but no less dramatically. Jim Bassett, a young Idaho cowboy, finds himself out of favor with Hetty Rhodes because a rival has accused him of rustling. Bassett, a Western Lochinvar, wins Hetty back at a Christmas dance, and the couple elope that night.

Travis, hero of "The Watchman," also wins an Idaho girl, but not so quickly nor so easily. Travis watches the walls and gates of a new irrigation ditch that has sprung dozens of leaks under the eyes of several former watchmen—perhaps because their eyes were occupied in looking for Nancy Lark, beautiful daughter of a nearby rancher. In convincing detail, Mrs. Foote describes how Travis constantly prowls the ditch, how he will not allow himself rest to talk at great length with Nancy, and yet how sorely he is tempted to forget the ditch and woo the girl. His devotion to duty pays a bitter bonus: he catches Nancy's father digging a hole in the ditch and forces the old man to help him fill it. Before Travis has a chance to report Lark's misdeed, the company fires him and old man Lark dies. Later, when Nancy discovers her father's guilt, she asks the company to reinstate Travis. He is reinstated. He returns and eventually marries Nancy. "The Watchman" deals with the formula of Mrs. Foote's early novels more skillfully; in this case the ground-swell is the young couple's love which overcomes the barrier between them.

The Cup of Trembling, and Other Stories (1895) continued the somewhat melodramatic tendencies of *In Exile*. In "The Cup of Trembling," for example, Mrs. Foote wrote about two lovers, Jack and Esmée, who had retreated to a high mountain cabin to escape both public notice and the wrath of Esmée's husband. Jack's brother Sid comes to Idaho to find him, but when he arrives at the cabin, Jack is not there, and Esmée, frightened, refuses to let him in. Sid wanders off and dies from exposure. Jack's reaction to the death is to assure Esmée, "You did not do it. I did not do it. It happened—to show us what we are" (p. 69). Having brought the lovers to this pass, Mrs. Foote ended their torment: Esmée is swept away in an avalanche. In spite of such contrived effects as the avalanche, the story is an interesting study of the joys and the tedium of forbidden love in a high mountain cabin.

The question of tragic love also provides the theme for "Maverick," one of Mrs. Foote's best short stories. An Eastern college student in Idaho as part of his tour of the West tells how Maverick loves Rose, daughter of stationmaster Gilroy. The Gilroys raised Maverick after Indians had killed his family and mutilated his face. Rose, who cannot stand Maverick's grotesque appearance, runs away with a Swede. As Sheriff of Lemhi County, Maverick pursues the couple and shoots Rose's lover, a man he had saved from frostbite the year before. Rose rides off into the lava fields near Craters of the Moon, a region so desolate the college student says of it, " 'This is where hell pops,' an old plainsman feelingly described it, and the suggestion is perfect" (p. 94). The men search for Rose, but she is never found. "The Black Lava fields," according to Mary Lou Benn, "symbolize the moving forces of matter caught in suspension; the girl's life, like that of the lava, has run its rough and rugged course, and she, too, is caught by the forces of nature" (p. 111).

Phebe Underhill, the heroine of "On a Side Track," is also greatly influenced by forces beyond her control. She and her Quaker father travel on the Omaha-to-Portland train to stay with her sister in Boise. Heavy snows sidetrack the train near the Idaho-Wyoming border just long enough for Charles Ludovic to win Phebe's heart. Assured of Phebe's affection, Ludovic tells her that he is being taken to Pocatello to stand trial for murder. Accused by a foul-mouthed lout of illicit relations with his friend's wife, Ludovic had fought his accuser and shot him with his own gun. Ludovic, acquitted at the trial, goes to Boise to see whether Phebe's first feelings of love survived the telling of his story. The two marry. "The case is in her hands now. She may punish, she may avenge, if she will; for Ludovic is the slave of his own remorseless conquest. But Phebe has never discovered that she was wronged" (p. 173).

Meta in "The Trumpeter" is more unlucky in love than Phebe, Rose, or Esmée. Daughter of a Hudson's Bay trapper and a Bannock Indian woman, Meta secretly marries Henniker, trumpeter for K Company at Fort Hall, Idaho. Transferred to Fort Custer, Montana, Henniker leaves Meta pregnant at Fort Hall. After her son is born, Meta takes the baby by train to Montana. She secures free passage by dressing as an Indian woman, but once off the train she finds that no one will give her a ride. She walks thirty miles in winter weather from the station to the fort. Henniker, just discharged, sees her on the way to the station, but he ignores her and then, as salve for his conscience, gives the stage driver a gold piece to give her. Meta dies, but the baby survives and is adopted by the Meadows family, Meta's foster family at Fort Hall.

Curiously, the story does not end at this point. Seven years pass, and Henniker becomes a degenerate bum and rabble rouser. He joins the contingent of Coxey's Army marching through Idaho and is arrested with his comrades. Mrs. Meadows and Henniker's son see him among the prisoners, but Mrs. Meadows does not tell the boy his father stands before them. After his release, Henniker drowns himself in the Snake River. Mrs. Foote's compassion for Meta is similar to Helen Hunt Jackson's concern for Indians, but it contrasts sharply with the former's contempt for Coxey's Army: "It seemed as if it might be time to stop laughing and gibing and inviting the procession to move on, when a thousand or more men, calling themselves American citizens, were parading their idleness through the land as authority for lawlessness and crime, and when our sober regulars had to be called out to quell a Falstaff's army" (pp. 250-251).

"The Trumpeter" implies that an Indian maid's "wild innocence" is victimized by the same dissolute character, the same decadent and idle forces promoting labor unrest. Though Mrs. Foote's technique had been steadily improving, it seems fortunate that she allowed herself half a decade's respite before she again published serious adult fiction. *The Little Fig-Tree* stories appeared in 1899, but these children's tales, mostly sentimental sketches or moral fables, had been written earlier. *The Cup of Trembling* marks the end of Mrs. Foote's early period. Characteristic of these early works is some sort of romance, usually complicated by placing one lover figuratively in the House of Montague and making the other a Capulet. The Western setting functions in the early works as first a barren backdrop to emphasize the drama, but later as a force in its own right often controlling the characters.

In the first years of the new century, Mrs. Foote's style matured; she abandoned for the most part the Romeo-Juliet formula, and she showed to greater effect her understanding of Western character and setting. The melodrama of some of the early works is notably diminished or absent; and many of her twentieth-century works probe the nature of parent-child relationships.

As the title of *The Prodigal* (1900) indicates, Mrs. Foote was especially concerned with what we now call the generation gap. Clunie Roberts, the prodigal son of the title, enters the doors of a prestigious San Francisco firm, Bradshaw and Company. A sorry sight clad in rags, Clunie begs the company to loan him a stake; his father, a wealthy New Zealand merchant, does considerable business with Bradshaw's firm; so Clunie guarantees that a loan to him would be repaid by his father. Morton Day, the employee who deals with Clunie, cannot give him more than fifty cents a day because of a company policy assuring protection against confidence men. As soon as Clunie's father writes to verify his identity, the company will grant the money. Clunie's father responds by asking the company to grant Clunie no more than his fifty-cents *per diem.* Not content with this parental parsimony, Clunie begins with Morton Day's help a small rowing business in the harbor.

Modest prosperity rewards Clunie and Morton. Bradshaw asks

Day to check the human cargo of a ship bearing 1,500 coolies illegally brought from China. Clunie and Day discover that the ship carries smallpox and must be quarantined. The ship's captain persuades Clunie to smuggle his pregnant wife ashore. The mother dies, and the surviving baby is given to the care of a beautiful aunt. To improve his financial condition, Clunie sells his harbor business and becomes a member of Bradshaw and Company. His proposal to Annie Dunstan, the beautiful aunt, is imminent.

Clunie's ordeal continues, however, when a ground-swell from his past almost overwhelms him. He finds a familiar looking woman with a small child booking passage on the *Parthenia*. The woman is actually his Mexican fiancée from St. Lucas, where he was stranded in Mexico before he came to California. Clunie learns that the *Parthenia* has less chance of floating than a Swiss cheese, so he takes the difficult action of finding his ex-fiancée and of convincing her to leave the ship. She does leave it. She also tells Clunie about her marriage to a ship's steward.

Unfortunately, one of Annie Dunstan's servants has told her mistress that Clunie boarded the ship. Thinking he has left without a word, Annie watches the *Parthenia* sail out the Golden Gate and suddenly sink. Running frantically to call help, she sees Clunie and Mort also running for help. Later Annie consents to marry Clunie, and he announces his intention to take his new bride to visit his father. Like the old man of Christ's parable about the prodigal son, Clunie's father says he will receive him with joy.

Among many other things, the West served as training school for prodigal sons; but in this novel, Mrs. Foote avoids overdoing exotic or romantic aspects of the situation. Most of the story is told from the point of view of Morton Day, a native New Englander whose assessments and reactions are finely imagined. Day and the reader notice that San Francisco has little society in the Eastern sense. In contrast to some of Mrs. Foote's earlier works, this social vacuum does not create a chaos or wilderness inhospitable to women. The city atmosphere evoked compares favorably with that of Norris' *McTeague,* which was published the year before *The Prodigal* appeared. The element missing from Mrs. Foote's novel is a more thoroughly developed idea of Clunie's father, a man who apparently believed the American West a place fit to develop his son's character.

The Desert and the Sown (1902) begins with "A Council of the Elders," Col. Middleton and Mrs. Emily Bogardus. Their children, Paul Bogardus and Moya Middleton, plan to marry soon. The couple seem to suit each other except that Paul wants to devote his life to the poor, and Moya wants him to devote it all to her. To explain his convictions to Moya and to refute her father's charge that he is "just a boy full of transcendental moonshine" (p. 15), Paul tells Moya the story of his parents. They eloped because his mother's father could not abide the idea of allowing his daughter Emmy to marry the hired hand, Adam Bogardus. Seeking their fortune in Idaho, the runaways encountered misfortune when they became separated. Unable to find her husband, Emily returned East—not to her father who had disinherited her, but to her uncle. Both old men left their estates to Emily and her children.

Having explained these reasons for his compassion for the lower class poor, Paul leaves with a hunting party going into the woods north of Challis. Heavy snows threaten to seal the hunters into the mountain valley; so they hurry back. Old Packer John's horse slips on ice and hurts his rider. Paul volunteers to stay and watch over him in a nearby cabin while the others go for help. Weak and out of food after weeks in the cabin, the two men learn they are father and son. Adam "Packer John" Bogardus tells Paul that when he tried to find Emily after they were separated, a lewd stationmaster enraged him with obscene taunts. Berserk, Adam broke the man's back, then ran into the sage desert to hide. After this tale is ended and the two men begin to learn how to accept each other and how to face imminent death, help arrives.

When they return to Boise, Emily Bogardus at first refuses to recognize the grizzled old packer as her lost husband; so Packer John again vanishes into the sage. As soon as Paul and Moya marry, they search for the old man. Packer John spends some time at a hot springs health ranch in Bruneau Valley and then finds a job on a cattle train headed to Chicago. Befuddled, the old man plans to return to his family's burial ground near the Hudson River.

Paul, Moya, and Emily also return to that area. The young couple have a child and stay with Emily at the old family home. Emily's father had died an embittered old man almost isolated in a prison-like garret room of the old family house, and the servants have since believed the room is haunted. In fact one of the hired men thinks he sees something in the room, but too frightened to look, he just locks the door. Almost a week later, Paul and Moya's child ventures near the room and draws attention to something inside. That "something" is the stinking, emaciated shell that remains of Adam Bogardus. Recognizing her mistake in Idaho, Emily now acknowledges that he is her husband and cares for him. Her care is too late; Adam soon dies uttering her name.

The old man's death serves as a powerful symbol of the cruelty wrought by the castes and classes of society. Mrs. Foote took the title from the eleventh stanza of Edward Fitzgerald's translation of the *Rubaiyat* of Omar Khayyám:

> With me along the strip of Herbage strown,
> That just divides the desert from the sown,
> Where name of Slave and Sultán is forgot—
> And Peace to Mahmúd on his golden Throne!

The change in Mrs. Foote's attitude from the contempt expressed for Coxey's Army in *The Cup of Trembling* to her compassion here seems the result of a more mature conception of man and society. The ordeal of parents and their children in *The Desert and the Sown* grants to them after great expense the vision to see through artificial barriers of class. The achievement of such a vision concerned most realists, and Mrs. Foote says in this novel, "Reality has its own convincing charm, not inconsistent with plainness or even with commonness. To know it is to lose one's taste for toys of the imagination" (pp. 133-134). Mrs. Foote succeeds when she is faithful to this dictum, but parts of *The Desert and the Sown* suffer from the sense of being too obviously transitions to effect the transfer of characters from one scene to another.

What Mrs. Foote tried to achieve in *The Desert and the Sown* is somewhat like the voyage theme of a Defoe novel or of Guthrie's *The Big Sky,* novels in which the protagonist leaves civilization because of a failure to conform or to succeed; he enters a wilderness, a colony, or a frontier where the rules allow greater freedom; but he finally succumbs to the home pull and returns to a society that seems constrictive in contrast to the freedoms of the wilderness. The final scenes of *The Desert and the Sown* are similar to the close of *The Prairie* (1827) by James Fenimore Cooper. Old Natty Bumppo dies in the middle of an Indian camp on the plains; his final word is "Here!" In contrast Packer John dies in bed in his home country, and his last word is his wife's name. Natty's death-shout reaffirms his transitional social status; Packer John's indicates both the success and the failure of civilization–*i.e.,* the love nourished by family and the hatred engendered by class.

A Touch of Sun, and Other Stories (1903) continued to explore questions of family, class, and parental responsibility. The title story describes the anguish of Mrs. Margaret Thorne, who discovers that her son Willy has become engaged to Helen Benedet, a rich young woman who lives under the shadow of an elopement with a cowboy desperado. Helen comes to Mrs. Thorne to explain what led to her impetuous act and why she has not told

Willy of her past. Helen also wants to break the engagement, but Willy arrives, says he knows of her past, and convinces her to marry him anyway. This action takes place at the Asgard mine in California's Sacramento Valley during a heat wave.

Idaho's Snake River Valley provides the setting for "The Maid's Progress," a study of what people actually think and feel in contrast to what circumstances seem to require them to feel. Reverend Withers and his niece Daphne Lewis have come to Pilgrim's Station near Decker's Ferry to make the arrangements for placing a fountain in memory of the minister's son John, who was killed there. Thane, their guide, plays the part of John's best friend. The natural physical forces of the sage desert work to destroy the minister's idealized illusions: Daphne and Thane confess that they were never to John what the Reverend supposed. The old man also has to hear Thane's declaration of love for Daphne and her promise to meet him in the town of Bliss. The "brute oblivion" of "miles of desert, days of desert" (p. 126) becomes, like the desert of Sinai, a land of revelations.

To Mrs. Valentin of San Francisco, the West of 1898 remains largely the cultural vacuum she had found it on moving there years ago. She thinks no Western city can offer her daughter Elsie the polish and refinement to be found in the East, so the two become "Pilgrims to Mecca." Elsie does not share her mother's views of the values of Mrs. Barrington's private school and would be satisfied to stay in San Francisco, but to please her mother, Elsie sacrifices her desire to stay home. At Chicago the ladies encounter their bishop, who had been transferred from San Francisco. He tells them that Billy Constant, Elsie's boy friend, has been killed with the Rough Riders at San Juan. Mrs. Valentin sees how deeply the news touches Elsie, how empty and cold Mrs. Barrington's school will seem. They return to San Francisco, which Mrs. Valentin now knows is more home than the "Mecca" of her earlier homesickness. In contrast to the sad ending, Mrs. Foote gives a humorous touch to the opening scenes of the story.

Mrs. Valentin notices another mother and daughter on the train; she is certain they are Eastern women and keeps pointing them out to Elsie to prove the values of an Eastern education. These women, it turns out, are also Californians.

"The Harshaw Bride" is also humorous. The situation resembles Harry Leon Wilson's *Ruggles of Red Gap* (1915) in that someone impeccably British finds herself almost overnight in the American West. Kitty Comyn, the English girl, arrives in Bisuka, Idaho, to marry Micky Harshaw. He fails to meet the train, but his cousin Cecil is there. Kitty stays with the Tom Dalys and learns that Micky does not want to marry her but that Cecil does. Cecil's proposal fails to win Kitty, but he interests Tom Daly in a scheme to build an electric plant at Thousand Springs. Mrs. Daly, who narrates the story, arranges a paid position for Kitty on the trip to Thousand Springs. On the way, the party passes Micky Harshaw's ranch and learns he has married his biggest creditor. Uncle George Harshaw, a widower, sends word of his intention to atone for his son Mickey's conduct by marrying Kitty himself. The poor girl, now desperate, still scoffs at Cecil's repeated proposal. Mrs. Daly reconciles Kitty and Cecil when she reveals an incident to Kitty proving that Cecil has indeed loved her for years. Convinced, she finally becomes "The Harshaw Bride."

Mrs. Foote's "How the Pump Stopped at the Morning Watch," published in *The Century* in 1899, did not appear in *A Touch of Sun*. Wallace Stegner, who included the story in his collection of *Selected American Prose,* surmised that Mrs. Foote felt that her rendition of the Cornish miners was inadequate (p. 119). The story tells how an old watchman and the wheel of a great mine pump meet their end together: the old man hit by a mine car in his distracted wandering, the wheel broken after years of strain and fatigue. Stegner includes excerpts from Mrs. Foote's letters describing the real incidents on which the story is based.

Mrs. Foote did not continue to work the humorous vein she

had struck in "The Harshaw Bride," and she did not pursue what Stegner has called "the only serious writing after Bret Harte to deal with mining-camp society, and virtually the only serious fiction which has dealt with the camps from intimate knowledge" (*Selected American Prose,* p. 117). Instead of writing more humorous fiction or more novels and stories dealing with mining-camps, Mrs. Foote turned next to historical fiction. The desire to write fiction based on history, the attempt "to balance the claims of past and present," as Jay Martin has put it (*Harvests of Change,* p. 137), seized many realists around the turn of the century. Cable, Garland, Stowe, Wilkins, and Jewett wrote historical romances, and some realists such as Edward Eggleston became historians. Mrs. Foote's interest centered on history's influence on character and family. The single, limited conflicts that tested lovers in her earlier works gave way to broad watersheds of history; the lovers' ordeal became correspondingly greater, the fictional background richer and more panoramic.

The Royal Americans (1910) follows the life of Catherine Yelverton, daughter of a soldier in the King's Army, from her birth on the eve before Montcalm took Oswego (August 12, 1756) to her marriage following the American Revolution. Catherine's mother dies shortly after her daughter's birth, and the infant is raised by a relative of her father, a Presbyterian minister named Deyo. Catherine's youth in rural, frontier New York exposes her to children of lower social station, particularly Bassy Dunbar, "son of a thief." Upon her adolescence is thrust a foster sister, Charlotte, a white but "savage" girl whom Col. Yelverton has rescued from Indian captivity. Catherine must also cope with her father's unsuccessful wooing of a young lady who finds Charlotte too much to accept. As young adults, Bassy and Catherine are attracted to each other, but Catherine gets engaged to someone else, and Bassy marries Charlotte to save her and Col. Yelverton from false and slanderous imputations. Catherine later breaks her engagement. When the fighting between Americans and British begins, Bassy joins rebel ranks. Col. Yelverton and Catherine, royalist sympathizers in the midst of patriots, maintain a discreet neutrality; but Charlotte defies her husband by aiding the Redcoats. Bassy is forced to arrest Col. Yelverton and to send his wife and Catherine to British lines. The two young women are reconciled and help each other at the Battle of Saratoga, during which Charlotte is killed. After the war, Bassy and Catherine marry and bring Col. Yelverton back from Canada to his old estates.

As this summary suggests, Mrs. Foote painted her picture on a broad canvas. Her research seems thorough, relying heavily on such primary sources as Baroness Riedesel's journals. From the historical materials Mrs. Foote makes a mosaic of opposing forces: Quakers vs. Presbyterians, Indians vs. whites, loyalists vs. revolutionists, high class vs. low class. Her treatment of these conflicts grants the complexity of the situations, but she still evaluates them in moral terms. For example, she scores white policy and conduct in the Indian wars; she shows how many loyalists needlessly suffered at the hands of patriots because of "Certain acts they [men in arms] are forced to perform; and friction between a man's nature and his duty is apt to heat up his way of doing it" (p. 383). Mrs. Foote may have intended a parallel between the welter of conflicting interests in revolutionary times and the social ferment and unrest during her own era of massive immigration and rapid change.

Her next work, *A Picked Company* (1912), also used the framework of historical fiction to trace the effects of change. In this novel not so many conflicts of interest arise; the problem for the characters and for the author is created by one person, Stella Mutrie. In the early 1840's eighteen-year-old Stella comes from Jamaica to live with her New England uncle and aunt, Alvin and Silence Hannington, and their daughter Barbie. Stella's beauty wins her many suitors and finally one rich fiancé. She breaks that engagement, however, when she sees Capt. Bradburn, the man who will guide Rev. Yardley's wagon train to Oregon. Though Bradburn is a married man, he has an affair with Stella when the pilgrims leave Independence. When Stella's pregnancy becomes too obvious to ignore and she refuses to express guilt or sorrow, Rev. Yardley banishes her from the train. His son Jimmie, who really loves Barbie Hannington, agrees to take Stella hundreds of miles back to Fort Hall for the winter. After the two have left the train, Bradburn confesses his responsibility for Stella's condition, resigns as guide, and leaves in pursuit of his lover. Jimmie refuses to surrender Stella and kills Bradburn in a duel. Informed by Bradburn that the wagon train expects his return, Jimmie takes Stella back to her uncle. She suffers a miscarriage after all the forced riding.

Once in Oregon, Stella continues to cause trouble by trying to lure a steadfast family farmer to join her in a search for some gold deposits that one of Bradburn's friends has told her about. The farmer refuses to join her; so Stella runs away. She becomes the mistress of the Hudson's Bay Company factor at Yerba Buena (San Francisco). When he dies and the gold rush begins, Stella is reduced to prostitution. In 1854 she tries to go straight again by marrying a good man, but her husband, noting her continued drinking and gambling, kills her and himself to save their unborn child from suffering. The novel ends with a description of how Jimmie Yardley and his bride, Barbie Hannington, prosper at farming in Oregon.

Within this outline, Mrs. Foote lets us see that for the New England Presbyterians Stella is a greater ordeal than is the vast Western wilderness. The Hanningtons must stand by her because she is family, but they dislike Stella almost as much as they love her. Of the others who are hurt by Stella's caprices, the Yardleys suffer most. Into a community of sacred ideals and sacred love, Rev. Yardley has permitted Bradburn and Stella, whose profane love destroys the harmony of the enterprise. Jimmie tries to save his father from the consequences of his judgments by protecting Stella, but she returns only harm for good.

All these troubles stem from the lack of any moral fiber in Stella's character: "This had been [Stella's] quarrel with existence: that you cannot pluck the rose of each situation without encountering the thorns" (p. 382). Part of this moral vacuity the narrator attributes to Stella's motherless condition, but most of the blame is placed on her Southern upbringing. The New Englanders, though perhaps too reserved, harsh, and inflexible, live inspired with some purpose; in contrast to these builders, Stella gambles for high passion, pleasure, and adventure.

The first part of *A Picked Company* lives as an imaginative, though limited, rendition of wagons West. All the characters head West in pursuit of their dreams, and all of them get what they wanted and are punished with their own fulfilled desires. Rev. Yardley wants to be among the first to bring God's word to Oregon; he does become a pioneer, but to do so he has to trust Bradburn, whose affair with Stella shakes the foundations of the minister's picked company. The novel's second part attempts to show how well all but Stella accept the thorns with the roses of their dreams. The attempt fails because Mrs. Foote follows Stella's descent in a narrative description too loose and cursory, and because we feel so little the effects of the westward trek upon the Yardleys and Hanningtons after Silence dies. If *A Picked Company* finally fails as a novel, parts of it remain memorable, particularly Bradburn's speech about the exploitation of pioneer women (p. 194).

In her last three novels, Mrs. Foote returned to events of her own lifetime. Yet these events seemed already matters of a bygone era. Gilder, her old editor, had died in 1909, and his wife Helena, Mary's closest friend, died in 1916. James and Howells either disappeared from public attention or came under vicious attacks of anti-Victorian critics like H. L. Mencken. Wister's *The Virginian* had taken its place as the *exemplum* of Western fiction. In the preface to *The Valley Road* (1915), Mrs. Foote acknowledged this change in public taste: "The author knows that her readers by now must be chiefly the old friends who read her books when she and they were young."

Mrs. Foote's old friends undoubtedly recognized the setting of *The Valley Road;* the story is set in the Sacramento Valley. Also apparent in this novel is Mrs. Foote's growing concern with relations between parents and children. Hal Scarth manages the Torres Tract; his brother-in-law Thomas Ludwell is a San Francisco businessman. Their children, Tom and Engracia Scarth and Clare Ludwell, represent the family hope and pride. Young Tom works as an engineer in Korea, where he falls in love with Mary Gladwyn. Before he can propose, he must return to California because of his father's failing health. Hal dies, and Tom takes his place as manager. When Gifford Cornish, an employee of the interests that own the Torres Tract, comes to investigate the Tract, Engracia falls in love with him. The feeling is mutual, but when Engracia receives a false report of Cornish's relations with his employer's wife, she says she will never marry him. Clare Ludwell complicates the situation with her infatuation for Tom Scarth. These love affairs come to a standstill until the great San Francisco Earthquake of 1906 brings everyone together. At the request of her parents, Tom finds Mary Gladwyn, who is nursing Dalby Morton (a playboy in love with Clare Ludwell) after his appendectomy, and the three go to the Torres Tract, where Engracia and her mother welcome them. Clare soon arrives there too. Tom and Mary and Gifford and Engracia settle differences, but Clare and Dalby attempt an elopement that fails pathetically. The first two couples marry, and Clare and Dalby will be allowed to marry if they can wait two years.

Though easily described, these love affairs are ordeals both for the lovers and for their parents. The novel's basic theme, "the understanding of one generation [does not] fit the needs of the next" (p. 352), bears an intentional similarity to the theme of George Meredith's *The Ordeal of Richard Feverel,* a book that provides a common interest for Gifford and Engracia. Both Meredith and Mrs. Foote recognize how painful, unpredictable, and occasionally uncontrollable love can be, and how parents complicate their children's love through direct interference, or lack of it, and through heredity and training. Though some ordeal seems so often unavoidable, Mrs. Foote spells out what should and what should not be at stake: "Heaven, we are told, lies about us in our infancy, and heaven knows it is not our dreams and the foolishness they lead to we wish to forget when we are old, but the mornings when we woke to the cock-crow of reality, and saw life in its baldness and its risks with a heart full of fear, and spake hard truths, not truth, to those we loved, and quenched their dreams and parted with our own in the name of this world's prudence" (p. 17). As in Mrs. Foote's earlier works, the Western ordeals are followed by a return to the East; Caroline Scarth and Anna Ludwell, the mothers, spend their old age in New England.

Mrs. Foote's final two novels are her best. *Edith Bonham* (1917) is narrated by the title character, a young lady who closely resembles Mrs. Foote's friend Helena De Kay Gilder, to whom the novel is dedicated. Motherless Edith lives in New York with her very Bohemian father. At the Cooper School of Design she meets Anne Aylesford, a farm girl from the Hudson River region. Anne, whose situation resembles that of Mrs. Foote, marries Douglas Maclay, a Canadian engineer who takes her to Idaho, where he owns a mine near Silver City in the Owyhees. The Maclays reside in Boise and have several children. Those four years of the Maclays' prosperity have not treated Edith well: her father, commissioned to paint the ballroom of a new mansion, has decided he must go to Tahiti to get the right scene, and his friend, Capt. Nashe, has decided to accompany him. Unable to afford the journey or to stomach Nashe, Edith asks Anne whether she would like help with her children. Anne begs Edith to come West immediately.

On arriving in Idaho, Edith learns of Anne's death. Anne's children need care—Douglas Maclay's mining activities keep him in Silver City; so he cannot give them love and attention. Edith agrees to care for the children. Problems develop. Dick Grant, Maclay's assistant, shows signs of falling in love with Edith. Maclay never appears long enough or frequently enough to give Edith the direction and reassurance she wants. Douglas trusts her, though; he asks her to design Anne's gravestone. His trust is shaken when his daughter Phoebe wanders off and plays with a dirty neighbor child who exposes her to scarlet fever. While the children play, Edith sits engrossed in G. W. Cable's *The Grandissimes.* Maclay's daughter does get scarlet fever, but he chooses to overlook Edith's quasi-negligence and entrusts her with the responsibility of nursing Phoebe in a quarantined home on the mesa.

Isolated by the remoteness of the mesa, by the quarantine, and by her feelings of guilt, Edith surrenders herself to nursing. Mrs. Foote's description of what was required of a nurse in those years shows how mentally and physically exhausting the task was. Yet the ordeal provides Edith with a temporary retreat from such disturbing questions as her feelings for Grant and Maclay, her position as an unmarried employee of a widower, her fears about the future. When Phoebe seems almost well and has learned to love Edith, Maclay brings news of her father's death at Papeete. The Western man, urged by his own feelings and by others' advice, proposes. Edith's shock and disgust at what she believes is his vulgarity run so deep that she almost leaves. Her departure comes months later at Maclay's request after she has learned town gossip about her relationship to Maclay and to a local doctor. Aware of some of this slander, Maclay asks her to take his children East to his wife's parents and to act as their governess.

Edith accepts Maclay's offer, knowing that a decision to raise his children places a barrier against her chance of finding a husband; she justifies the sacrifice by citing her love for Anne and for Phoebe and by referring to her ambivalent feelings for Douglas. In her Eastern haven, secure from the demands of the frontier, Edith probes her memories of her Boise experience deeply and sees in them the destruction of any innocent belief in a consistently benign and predictable world. "I hated it [the West]," she admits, "and so did Nanny [Anne]. But it 'haunted' us both. It has tremendous force, concealed somehow; things may happen any time, but you don't know what, nor where to expect them. It's like a sea sown with floating mines, innocent of its own terrors. You may go safe a hundred times and then you may strike something that explodes and you go out of sight" (p. 263). In trying to sort out her feelings for Westerner Maclay, Edith must also admit the failure of her Aunt Essie's marriage; a union for the sake of convenience and security, but one with so many voids —no love, no sharing—it is not without "its own terrors."

For four years Edith maintains an almost monastic existence, devoting herself to the Maclay children and to preparing her father's letters for publication. Douglas does not openly suggest marriage again, but in his many letters he "disguises" the proposal in obvious fables. When Mrs. Aylesford finally reads some of these fables and forces from Edith the full story, she writes to insist on Maclay's presence, and she tries to persuade Edith to forgive and marry him. Maclay says he will visit, but other sources say he may be coming East to take his children back for his wedding to a Miss Blair. However, Maclay's love for Edith has remained sure; he proposes again, and she accepts. They marry, settle in Boise, and have two more children.

Phoebe adds some "Later Words" about Edith's life. Phoebe claims that her stepmother was probably a better woman than her mother (something Edith obviously would not say). Edith had grown to like Boise more after her return: her circumstances had changed, and the town was becoming a small city. Phoebe also tells something about her own marriage. She concludes by mentioning that Edith died at the start of World War I, hating

Germany and hating American neutrality. One of her sons died fighting "over there." Phoebe's husband is there, and she tells us of her dream in which the Germans bomb Boise.

The note of anti-German rancor appears incongruous with the bulk of the novel. It is a forced way of showing the parallel between the testing of character in the West and the same ordeal in Flanders Field. What redeems the novel is that the journey West is not so liberally spiced with the romantic melodrama of her earlier works—it becomes rather an emergence into "a great bare land of sunshine [where] you learn the value of shadows" (p. 331)—a reality different from that in the East, simply a more intense crucible for the spirit. As such, the West confuses, tortures, isolates its immigrants; but it also grants them the products —not unalloyed—of such an alembic.

Edith Bonham's sacrifice of her Eastern sensibility and of her pride to the joys and burdens of her marriage makes a fitting prelude to the question of parental love and sacrifice in *The Ground-Swell* (1919). Edith tells her own story, and Mrs. Cope narrates *The Ground-Swell.* She and her husband, Col. Charley Cope, retire to Vallevista near Santa Cruz after forty-two years in the army. "A mother's thoughts at my age," admits Mrs. Cope, "are so often a review of her own mistakes with her children" (p. 43). The Copes have three daughters: Patty, their youngest, an army bride in the Philippines; Cecily, the oldest, married to a rich San Francisco playboy; and Katherine, single and living in New York. The old-age idyl of the Copes is disrupted by the ground-swell of emotions reaching them from their daughters' lives.

Most of the ground-swell comes from the two oldest daughters. Cecily, though beautiful, has a trivial, bourgeois sensibility; her husband's status and fortune form the core of her love for him, and Mrs. Cope is guilty of having encouraged the marriage for the same reasons. Bright, sensitive Katherine knew what sort of man her brother-in-law Peter Dalbert was before the marriage; she witnessed his disgusting behavior on the train and she felt hurt that her parents would give Cecily to Dalbert. Katherine has given herself only to altruistic pursuits: after attending Bryn Mawr she works in the New York ghettos. These two daughters decide to inspect their parents' refuge. Cecily objects to the isolation; Katherine finds it charming.

Katherine is also charmed by Tony Kayding, a young man who watches over a nearby old hotel. He, too, has sensitivity. Very much like Robinson Jeffers, he values the wild things of nature more than cities. Though the couple appreciate each other and Tony falls in love with Katherine, little seems to come of it until Mrs. Cope takes a hand. She knows, as is evident from her allusion to *The Ordeal of Richard Feverel,* how dangerous meddling in love affairs can be, but she excuses her matchmaking by saying she does not carry her experiments so far as Sir Austin Feverel does his. She carries hers far enough. Tony proposes, and Katherine refuses.

Mrs. Cope must bear the failure of her experiment. Katherine goes back to New York; Cecily has already returned to San Francisco. Before Mrs. Cope has fully recovered from her daughters' visit, she encounters her son-in-law, Peter Dalbert, struggling with a drunken slattern on a high promontory above a dangerous cliff. The woman slips at the edge, and Dalbert, out of fear for himself, refuses the effort to save her. Mrs. Cope soon has to deal with more than Dalbert's cowardice; when she demands that he be honest with Cecily, he disappears. Cecily, now pregnant, must undergo the ordeal of desertion.

The Copes can do little to ease Cecily's agony; so they go East to spend the winter with Katherine in New York. Cecily writes how she is helping Tony Kayding furnish a splendid new house at Vallevista. Dalbert also learns of Cecily's help, and when he accidentally encounters Mrs. Cope in New York, he accuses his wife of perfidy. Mrs. Cope's vigorous denial sends Dalbert home, where he tells his wife all he has done and begs forgiveness.

Cecily requires an ordeal of him; she sends him off to the World War in France.

At the same time, the elder Copes also undergo ordeals. They must cope with their "modern" daughter and her liberated friends, young women who smoke, who refuse to believe in "my country right or wrong," and who devote their lives to helping the poor and downtrodden. The Copes watch these idealists go off to France to help in the war effort. The old couple return to California and discover that the house Tony Kayding built is a gift to them. Tony's kindness, Peter Dalbert's success as an ace in the "Air Service," and news of Patty's return while her husband fights do little to help soften the blow of Katherine's death in France.

Mrs. Foote makes us understand the meaning of these parent-child ordeals by showing us how much Mrs. Cope is her family. The old mother realizes that the new generation will not be molded by every parental whim, but she also knows how much influence she does have, and she tries to use that to good effect. Unfortunately, Cecily has been spoiled and so suffers for her parents' indulgence and for her self-indulgence. Wishing to avoid Cecily's mistakes, Katherine sacrifices all happiness in fear of any indulgence. Patty's future lies with the army, a prospect at that time without much comfort.

In regional terms, the novel is ironic. Cecily, sissified and city-fied, lives in the West. Katherine, an outdoorish and active child of the West, leaves the happiness promised her there for a thankless altruistic quest in the East. The elder Copes retire at Point Del Refugio, but the coastal beauty, paradise in terms of what they desire in a place, provides no refuge from the rest of the world. The magnificence, beauty, and sense of freedom inherent in the Western landscape offer no immunity from the blows of the ground-swell, an image symbolic in the depth and unity it gives the book.

The ground-swell of Mrs. Foote's influence on her own time

may yet reach the shores of our age. If it does, her faults will be readily apparent. Especially in the earlier works, these weaknesses stand out: her genteel reticence, her sometimes melodramatic plots, her often wooden characters, her frequent failure to see the West as little more than a picturesque cultural vacuum to be endured out of necessity. If her work consisted of only these weaknesses, it would be insufferable to anyone but an antiquarian. One of the opportunities she overlooked is also apparent: she did not write a novel about Chinese, in spite of the fact that she knew many Chinese servants and merchants in the West. Her naive view of the labor question is another of her blind spots.

Her failures must be recognized, but so must her successes. She usually deals sensitively with the conditions of frontier life, emphasizing female anguish at being transplanted from the settled social world of the East to the barren cultural soil of the West, and yet recognizing (at least in her later works) that "it really pays to strip one's self down to 'food and fire and candle-light'; it is then, truly, God rests one's soul" (*The Ground-Swell,* p. 28). Though she sees no harm in mining and irrigation *per se,* she does speak out against the excessive greed that has in recent years denuded our forests, fouled our rivers, and poisoned our air. With the subtlety and uniqueness of the woman's point of view, her finest insight shows the complexity of the parent-child relationship. As Wallace Stegner said, "By no means a major figure, she is too honest to be totally lost" (*Selected American Prose,* p. xi).

In her candor, Mrs. Foote admitted that "The West is not to be measured by homesick tales from an Eastern point of view" (*The Last Assembly Ball,* p. 8). Her works do not so much measure the West—though she tried to avoid the easy, superficial depiction of "picturesque outward differences"—as they bring to life the experience of the Gibson girl *deracinée,* uprooted from New York salons and New England cottages and asked to make do with the social life of a Western mining camp. Her record of the West's "social genesis," her gradual realization that the West, too, could be home, adds its own significant measure of the period and of the Eastern sensibility brought West.

Selected Bibliography

Works by Mary Hallock Foote

NOVELS

The Led-Horse Claim: A Romance of a Mining Camp. Boston: J. R. Osgood, 1883.

John Bodewin's Testimony. Boston and New York: Houghton Mifflin, 1886.

The Last Assembly Ball and the Fate of a Voice. Boston and New York: Houghton Mifflin, 1889.

The Chosen Valley. Boston and New York: Houghton Mifflin, 1892.

Coeur d'Alene. Boston and New York: Houghton Mifflin, 1894.

The Prodigal. Boston and New York: Houghton Mifflin, 1900.

The Desert and the Sown. Boston and New York: Houghton Mifflin, 1902.

The Royal Americans. Boston and New York: Houghton Mifflin, 1910.

A Picked Company. Boston and New York: Houghton Mifflin, 1912.

The Valley Road. Boston and New York: Houghton Mifflin, 1915.

Edith Bonham. Boston and New York: Houghton Mifflin, 1917.

The Ground-Swell. Boston and New York: Houghton Mifflin, 1919.

COLLECTIONS OF FICTION

In Exile, and Other Stories. Boston and New York: Houghton Mifflin, 1894.

The Cup of Trembling, and Other Stories. Boston and New York: Houghton Mifflin, 1895.

The Little Fig-Tree Stories. Boston and New York: Houghton Mifflin, 1899.

A Touch of Sun, and Other Stories. Boston and New York: Houghton Mifflin, 1903.

UNCOLLECTED SHORT STORIES

"Cascarone Ball." *Scribner's Monthly,* 18 (August 1879), 614-17.

"A Story of the Dry Season." *Scribner's Monthly,* 18 (September 1879), 766-81.
"The Borrowed Shift." *Land of Sunshine,* 10 (December 1898), 12-24.
"How the Pump Stopped at the Morning Watch." *Century Magazine,* 58 (July 1899), 469-72. Rpt. in *Selected American Prose: The Realistic Movement, 1841-1900.* Ed. Wallace Stegner. New York: Holt, Rinehart and Winston, 1958. Pp. 116-27.
"The Eleventh Hour." *Century Magazine,* 71 (January 1906), 485-93.

SKETCHES

"A California Mining Camp." *Scribner's Monthly,* 15 (February 1878), 480-93.
"A Sea-Port on the Pacific." *Scribner's Monthly,* 16 (August 1878), 449-60.
"A Diligence Journey in Mexico." *Century Magazine,* 23 (November 1881), 1-14.
"A Provincial Capital of Mexico." *Century Magazine,* 23 (January 1882), 321-33.
"From Morelia to Mexico City on Horseback." *Century Magazine,* 23 (March 1882), 643-55.

MANUSCRIPTS

Most of Mrs. Foote's manuscripts are in collections at the University of California at Berkeley, the Harvard University Library, the Huntington Library, the New York Public Library, the Stanford University Library, and the Wisconsin Historical Society.

FORTHCOMING PUBLICATIONS

Professor Rodman Paul is preparing an edition of Mrs. Foote's "Reminiscences." Miss Rosamond Gilder is planning an edition of Mrs. Foote's letters.

BIBLIOGRAPHY

Etulain, Richard. "Mary Hallock Foote, 1847-1938." *American Literary Realism,* 5 (Spring 1972), 145-50.

BIOGRAPHICAL, CRITICAL, AND BACKGROUND MATERIALS

Armstrong, Regina. "Representative American Women Illustrators." *Critic,* 37 (August 1900), 131-41.

Benn, Mary Lou. "Mary Hallock Foote: Early Leadville Writer." *The Colorado Magazine,* 33 (April 1956), 93-108.

———. "Mary Hallock Foote in Idaho." *University of Wyoming Publications,* 20 (July 15, 1956), 157-78.

———. "Mary Hallock Foote: Pioneer Woman Novelist." Unpublished master's thesis, University of Wyoming, 1955.

Cady, Edwin H. *The Light of Common Day: Realism in American Fiction.* Bloomington and London: Indiana University Press, 1971.

Cody, Alpheus Sherwin. "Artist-Authors." *Outlook,* 49 (May 26, 1894), 910-11.

Davidson, Levette Jay. "Letters from Authors." *The Colorado Magazine,* 19 (July 1942), 122-25.

———, and Prudence Hostwick. *The Literature of the Rocky Mountain West.* Caldwell: Caxton, 1939.

Donaldson, Thomas. *Idaho of Yesterday.* Caldwell: Caxton, 1941.

Dufva, Diane. "Fact vs. Fiction: Leadville, Colorado, as a Setting for Fiction." Unpublished master's thesis, Kansas State University, 1966.

Etulain, Richard. "The New Western Novel." *Idaho Yesterdays,* 15 (Winter 1972), 12-17.

Foote, Arthur B. "Memoir of Arthur De Wint Foote." *Transactions of the American Society of Civil Engineers,* 99 (1934), 1449-52.

Gilder, Helena De Kay. "Mary Hallock Foote." *Bookbuyer,* 11 (August 18, 1894), 338-42.

Letters of Richard Watson Gilder. Ed. Rosamond Gilder. Boston: Houghton Mifflin, 1916.

Linton, W. J. "The History of Wood-Engraving in America: Part IV." *American Art and American Art Collections,* 1 (1899), 451-64.

Lummis, Charles F. "The New League for Literature and the West." *The Land of Sunshine,* 8 (April 1898), 206-14.

Martin, Jay. *Harvests of Change: American Literature, 1865-1914.* Englewood Cliffs, N. J.: Prentice-Hall, 1967.

Meyers, Harriet. "Mary Hallock Foote." Typescript in the Boise Public Library, August 1940.

Schopf, Bill. "The Image of the West in *The Century,* 1881-1889." *The Possible Sack* [University of Utah], 3 (March 1972), 8-13.

Smith, Herbert F. *Richard Watson Gilder.* New York: Twayne, 1970.

Smith, Robert Wayne. *The Coeur d'Alene Mining War of 1892: A Case Study of an Industrial Dispute.* Corvallis: Oregon State University Press, 1961.

Spence, Clark C. *Mining Engineers and the American West.* New Haven: Yale University Press, 1970.

Stegner, Wallace. *Angle of Repose.* Garden City, N. J.: Doubleday, 1971.

———, ed. *Selected American Prose: The Realistic Movement, 1841-1900.* New York: Holt, Rinehart and Winston, 1958.

Taft, Robert. *Artists and Illustrators of the Old West: 1850-1900.* New York: Scribner's, 1953.

Tomsich, John. *A Genteel Endeavor: American Culture and Politics in the Gilded Age.* Palo Alto: Stanford University Press, 1971.